The Littles

and the Summer Storm

The Littles

and the Summer Storm

Adapted by **Teddy Slater**
from *THE LITTLES AND THE BIG STORM*
by **John Peterson**
Illustrated by **Jacqueline Rogers**

SCHOLASTIC INC.
New York Toronto London Auckland Sydney
Mexico City New Delhi Hong Kong Buenos Aires

CRASH! BOOM! BANG!

Lightning flashed.

Thunder roared.

Lucy Little held

her tiny hands over

her tiny ears.

"Come on, Lucy!"

her brother, Tom, shouted.

"We have to get out of this storm."

Tom and Lucy ran

across the lawn.

The rest of the Littles

were waiting at their

secret doorway to

Mr. and Mrs. Bigg's house.

"I hope that wind doesn't blow this whole house away," Mrs. Little said.

The Little family lived

inside the walls of

the Bigg family's house.

The Littles were just
a few inches tall,
so there was plenty
of room for them there.

When the Biggs were home,

the Littles kept out of sight.

But now the Biggs were

away for the weekend, so

the Littles did not have to hide.

They were not afraid of

the Biggs' cat, Hildy.

She was their friend.

The rain came down all day.

Mr. Little began to worry.

"I hope the cellar

isn't flooding," he said.

"Let's go down and see," said Uncle Pete.

The Littles went down the
cellar stairs.

Uh-oh. Mr. Little was right.

There was water

all over the cellar floor.

"The drain must be

stopped up," said Mr. Little.

"I'd better swim out

and fix it, or soon

everything will be underwater."

"The drain is in the middle

of the floor,"

said Granny Little.

"That's a long way to swim."

"No one has to swim,"
Lucy said.
"We can build a raft with
Henry Bigg's Lincoln Logs
and *row* out there!"
Everyone liked Lucy's idea.

The Littles found the

Lincoln Logs in Henry Bigg's room.

They loaded five logs into

their tin-can elevator

and took them downstairs.

Everyone helped to get
the logs down the
cellar stairs.
It was hard work!

Then Tom and Lucy found

some rubber bands

to tie the logs together.

Granny went into the Biggs'
kitchen and came back
with two plastic spoons
to use as paddles.

At last, they were ready to go.

"All aboard!" Lucy sang out.

"Sorry, Lucy," Mr. Little said.

"There's only room for me,

and maybe Tom, on this raft."

"That's not fair!" Lucy cried.

"The raft was my idea."

Tears filled her eyes,

but no one noticed.

Lucy climbed to the top
of the cellar stairs.
Just above her head
was a large pipe.
It went all the way
across the room.

Far below the pipe,

the raft floated along.

Suddenly, Lucy got

another idea.

Lucy pulled herself onto the pipe.

Slowly, she inched

her way along it.

Then she leaned over

to get a better view. . . .

"Oops!"

Lucy fell head over heels.

"Help!" she yelled.

"Somebody save me!"

Tom and Mr. Little rowed toward
the sound of Lucy's voice.
But Lucy had disappeared
beneath the cold,
dark waves.

Suddenly, Lucy's head popped up.

"Look what I found,"

she called.

She was holding onto a wet rag.

"This is what was

clogging the drain."

"Grab my paddle, Lucy,"

Tom cried.

He pushed a plastic spoon

toward her.

Then Mr. Little pulled Lucy

onto the raft.

The Littles rowed back

to the stairs.

By the time they got there,

most of the water had

already gone down the drain.

The very next day,

the Biggs came home.

They had seen the storm

on the TV news.

Mr. and Mrs. Bigg
checked out their house
from top to bottom.
They could hardly
believe their eyes.

"I don't get it," said Mr. Bigg.

"The yard was such a mess,

but the house is fine."

"Yes," Mrs. Bigg agreed.

"Why, even the cellar

is as dry as a bone!"